In loving memory of my father,
Bernard Carl Seltzer

Thanks to Mom, the late Ted Geisel,
Kate Klimo, Cathy Goldsmith, Mike,
Lori, Justin, Kaitlyn, Sharon Simo,
Robert Thibodeau, Alan Cohen
and "the 12," Marirosa Donisi,
Chris Griffin, Alex Fox, and God

GROLIER
BOOK CLUB EDITION

BEGINNER BOOKS
A Division of Random House, Inc.
New York

http://www.randomhouse.com/

Library of Congress Cataloging-in-Publication Data
Seltzer, Eric.   Four pups and a worm / by Eric Seltzer.   p.   cm.
SUMMARY: When needing to solve a problem, the reader can call upon four
pups and a worm for help with anything from tying a tie to delivering bubbles.
ISBN: 0-679-87931-5 (trade). — ISBN 0-679-97931-X (lib. bdg.)
[1. Problem solving—Fiction.   2. Helpfulness—Fiction.   3. Stories in rhyme.]
I. Title.   PZ8.3.S4665Fo   1996   [E]—dc20   95-44115

Printed in the United States of America   10 9 8 7 6 5 4 3 2 1

4 PUPS and a WORM

by Eric Seltzer

4 PUPS and a WORM

4 Pups & A Worm
Headquarters
44 BONE BLVD.

When you cannot tie your tie—
no matter how you try...

When your chopper will not fly—
and you feel you want to cry...

When your car begins to steam—
and you're just about to scream...

And your mower starts to stall—
when your grass is ten feet tall.
Who are you going to call?

Call 4 Pups and a Worm.

They tie.

V-R-R-O-O-M

They fly.

They tow.

They mow—
those 4 Pups and a Worm.

A. J. sings.

Rex can dance.

Give this party crew a chance!

Digger knows dinosaurs.

Rex knows trees.

Goober's an expert
on ticks and fleas.

They plant flowers.

They pick up litter.

They'll even be
your baby-sitter!

Just call 4 Pups and a Worm.

If you need a bubble bath
and are down
to your last bubble—

call 4 Pups and a Worm.

(Delivering bubbles

is no trouble!)

Are they up to any task?

Here's what folks will often ask:

"Can they help me dry my toes?"

"Yes—and also blow your nose."

"How are they at scratching backs?"

"Good—and Rex can play the sax."

"How are they at zipping zippers?"
"They zip up AND down, those little nippers."

"Any good
at fixing leaks?"

"Leaks
and creaks

and even
squeaks!"

Who cleans?

Who sews?

If a pet frog
sounds like fun,

would 3 Cats and a Slug
lend you one?
(Never, no, never!
They're just not
that clever.)

Call 4 Pups and a Worm.

THEY LEND FROGS.

Sherm Worm handles
every call.

Winter,

spring,

summer,

fall.

One day, a call
came in to Sherm.
A call that made
the poor worm squirm.

Did Ernie Johnson
scrape his knee?

Did Shirley Chicken
spill her tea?

Did Bernice Bee
slip in the shower?

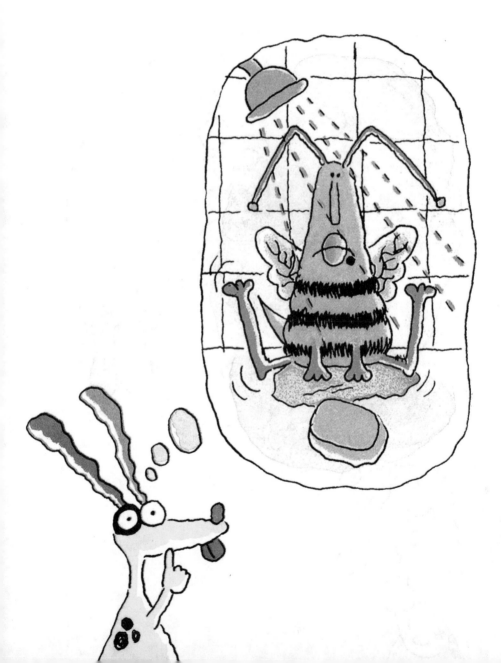

No, she got stuck
up in a flower.

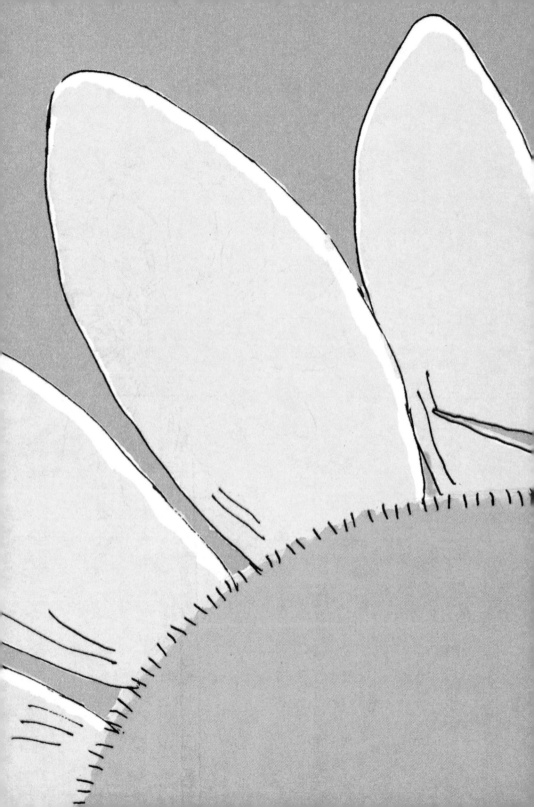

"HELP!" she cried.
"I'm stuck up here.
Get me out.
Oh dear, oh dear!"

So Rex got out

the 4 Pups' ladder.

In 7 minutes,
our team got at her!

Bernice was so happy,
she offered them money.

But the Pups and Sherm said,
"Pay us with honey."

So remember—
If you'd like
a piece of candy,
but there isn't
any handy,

DON'T call 8 Pigs and a Bat.

DON'T DO THAT!

Call 4 Pups and a Worm.

They like to help,
and that is why

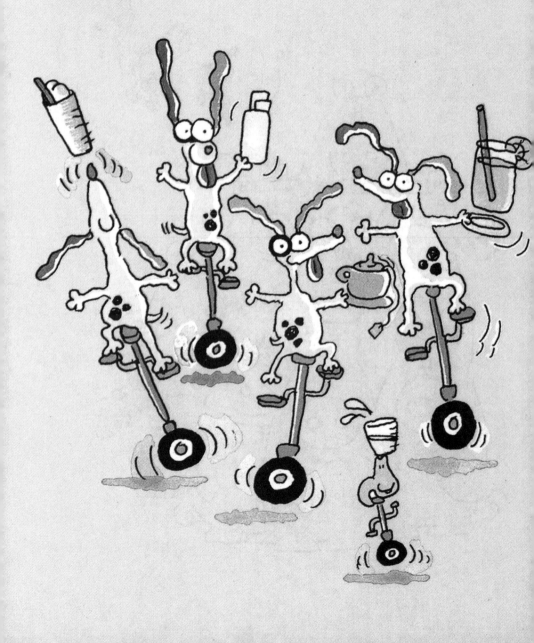

they hope you'll give
their team a try.

Good-bye!
(And don't forget to call
4 Pups and a Worm!)